THE PRANK

THE DO-OVER

THE PRANK

JEFFREY PRATT

darbycreek
MINNEAPOLIS

Darby Creek
A division of Lerner Publishing Group, Inc.
241 First Avenue North
Minneapolis, MN 55401 USA

For reading levels and more information, look up this title at www.lernerbooks.com.

Image credits: ub-foto/Shutterstock.com; VshenZ/Shutterstock.com.

Main body text set in Janson Text LT Std 12/17.5.
Typeface provided by Adobe Systems.

Library of Congress Cataloging-in-Publication Data

Names: Pratt, Jeffrey, 1967– author.
Title: The prank / Jeffrey Pratt.
Description: Minneapolis : Darby Creek, [2019] | Series: The do-over | Summary:
  Reeling from the repercussions of a prank gone wrong, Audrey takes the
  opportunity to do her day over, but doing so makes her see more about the day and
  forces her to make serious changes to how she decides to go forward.
Identifiers: LCCN 2018015838 (print) | LCCN 2018023034 (ebook) |
  ISBN 9781541541931 (eb pdf) | ISBN 9781541540309 (lb : alk. paper) |
  ISBN 9781541545526 (pb : alk. paper)
Subjects: | CYAC: Practical jokes—Fiction. | Guilt—Fiction. | High schools—Fiction.
  | Schools—Fiction.
Classification: LCC PZ7.1.P699 (ebook) | LCC PZ7.1.P699 Pr 2019 (print) | DDC
  [Fic]—dc23

LC record available at https://lccn.loc.gov/2018015838

Manufactured in the United States of America
1-45235-36617-9/10/2018

1

"We could maybe put bees in her locker. Like, lots of bees. *Angry* bees," Rachel suggested.

"Kinda extreme, don't you think?" Audrey shook her head. She loved her friends, but sometimes they got carried away. She knew she had to be the voice of reason as they plotted revenge against Hope Barcomb for the smallest of reasons. They were all gathered in Melicia's backyard around a small fire pit and, amazingly, were actually considering the angry bees plan. "No bees," Audrey added firmly, mostly for Rachel's sake.

"Whatever," Rachel sighed. "But we have to do something. Hope Barcomb has to be stopped."

"Here's a crazy idea," Audrey said. "How about: Ig. Nore. Her."

Rachel stood. "You weren't there. If you were, you would think we should do something too."

Audrey rolled her eyes. Then, she looked for some help from Melicia, who was sitting cross-legged on the front end of her lounge chair. Melicia was hunched over her laptop as usual. Her fingers moving rapidly over the keys.

"How bad was it?" Audrey asked.

"I don't know," Melicia said, not looking up from whatever she was working on. "The usual, I guess."

Audrey slid her gaze to Bryant, and he shrugged too. He was leaning back on his elbows, his long legs stretched out. "Yeah, the usual," he agreed.

"So," Audrey looked back at Rachel, "then it's not really a big deal. Why are we still talking about this?"

"Because how and when did *this* become 'the usual'?" Rachel asked. "Why does Hope Barcomb get to say and do whatever she wants?"

"She made a fart noise at you," Audrey replied.

"Yeah," Rachel said. "Every time I walk by. She's been doing it all week. It's gross and stupid. And, of course, all her stupid friends think it's the most hilarious thing they ever heard. And that's just one example—the *latest* example. Sheila Faller transferred out of school because of Hope. You know that, right? And have you somehow forgotten the time she got into *your* gym locker and filled *your* sneakers with hair gel?"

"Classic," Bryant smiled.

"Don't even start, Bryant." Rachel glared at him before turning back to Audrey. "Because I haven't forgotten. She's just an awful person."

"The Sheila Faller thing is a rumor. I think she had to move because her mom got a new job. And, as for the hair gel, that was more than two years ago. And it's kind of unimportant, all things considered. Why get into a thing with her?"

"She thinks she's a big deal because her dad is the dean of students," Rachel spat back.

Audrey shook her head. "She thinks she's a big deal because, at Clara Barton High, she *is* a big deal. Why get so upset over it?"

"I just think she's a bully," Rachel argued. "She makes her stupid comments and then says she was just joking. The number of times I've heard her ask 'Can't you take a joke?' is ridiculous. And since daddy's always got her back, the school's clearly not going to do anything about it. So someone else should."

"Okay, then do something," Audrey said. "Write a post about it for the blog. Not about her, specifically. But maybe something about bullying at the school. Or when 'joking around' can go too far or—"

"Boring," Rachel grunted.

Audrey laughed. "Apparently not to you. I think it could actually be a good article. And I bet the comments section would blow up."

Rachel shook off the idea. "No, what we should do is put something up on the blog about her specifically. Something nasty. Then tell her 'Just joking! Can't you take a joke?'"

For almost two years, the four of them had

run a blog that covered everything from the rising prices in the school cafeteria and phone-app reviews to "Top 8 Valentines' Day Ideas for the Terribly Truly Lonely." *The Espresso* had started as something to do one weekend but had turned into a regular thing where they took turns adding new posts every week: long essays about some social justice or news item by Audrey, reviews of some kind from Mel, Rachel's infamous Top 8 lists, and Bryant's funny cartoons—including an ongoing series called *The Pi Chronicles* about a one-eyed dog and his neighborhood friends.

It was surprising how much fun they had working on the blog. It was even more surprising how many people actually read it. It had basically become the unofficial news source of the school. And once kids started posting about it on social media, it even got a decent amount of attention beyond the school.

Part of the attention was from people trying to figuring out *who* at Clara Barton wrote the blog.

All posts were anonymous. And they used

some special software Melicia had found to conceal their location and real email addresses. Plus they usually used the local library computers instead of their own laptops to be on the safe side. All four friends played along like they had no idea who it was, either. When they all graduated next year and stopped posting, people would probably be able to narrow it down easily enough. But for now, Audrey thought it was a good idea to keep the blog more neutral, which meant not attacking one person specifically.

"Or we post something about her that just *might* be true?" Melicia suggested, looking up from her laptop. "Enough to get people talking."

"Yes!" Rachel squealed. "I love it!"

"You're both terrible," Audrey said, hoping her dismissive attitude would shut them down.

Bryant perked up. "I don't know. That could be kind of cool. I mean, what's the point of having an anonymous blog if we can't use it for stuff like this?"

Audrey raised an eyebrow. "You mean lies? We've never put fake stuff on the blog before."

"What about Bryant's cartoons?" Rachel pointed out. "Or your, ah, satiric articles about wizard schools and zombie apocalypses."

"Those are jokes," Audrey corrected. "Satire. It's all just for fun."

"Then write *this* one for fun," said Melicia.

"Hang on, how is it that *I'm* now the one responsible for writing this?"

"You *are* the best writer . . ." Melicia said.

"Guilty as charged," Audrey grinned. "But no thanks."

"Then I'll write it," Rachel declared.

"I vote yes," Melicia added, popping her head up again.

"Ditto," said Bryant.

Audrey was clearly outvoted three to one. But she wasn't quite ready to give up on trying to show them what a bad idea this was. "Then why stop there?" she asked sarcastically. "Why not aim higher? Let's go for her dad."

Bryant's eyes widened in the firelight. "Dean Barcomb?"

"Sure," Audrey said. She kept hoping they'd see how ridiculous they were being. After all, nobody had a problem with the dean, other than the fact that his daughter was obnoxious. "Take them both down at the same time. Write something about how, I don't know, he faked his resume and whatnot. Lied about his diploma or work experience. That kind of thing."

"Yes!" Rachel cheered.

Audrey tried to backtrack. "No! It was another joke. I was trying to—"

Rachel stopped her, grabbing both her shoulders. "You, Audrey Zimmer, are a total genius. And we should totally do it."

Audrey scowled. "Hope's right. You guys really can't take a joke. Forget it."

"Too late," Rachel replied. "You already put it out there. Can't forget now."

"I've found a couple of his social media accounts . . ." Melicia typed away at her laptop keys with even greater speed than before. "And a professional jobs and business connections account." She looked up with genuine joy. "He posted his resume."

A sick worry coiled in Audrey's stomach.

"If we get caught, we'll be expelled. Maybe even worse. Sued or something."

"*If* we get caught," Melicia said. "And we won't. The blog's completely anonymous and untraceable. No one will ever know who wrote it. No one's getting in trouble and no one's getting sued."

Bryant was still grinning, excited. "We should say that he takes bribes, like fifty bucks gets you off probation. We could even make up a criminal record with mugshots and all. Here, look!"

He held up a rough cartoon of Mr. Barcomb's mugshot. It had numbers below his face and all. The drawing was already spot on and he'd worked on it for about two minutes. Audrey knew the finished one would be a masterpiece.

"Um, maybe stick to your zombie drawings," Audrey said.

"I prefer vampires," he answered. "I wonder if Mr. Barcomb would make a good vampire." He went back to his sketch pad, his face mostly lost in the darkness.

Audrey shook her head. Now things were

just getting ridiculous. Who would believe Mr. Barcomb was a vampire? The idea of him even taking bribes was, frankly, just as absurd. But suddenly Audrey saw a sliver of an opportunity. Bryant's idea might actually be a good thing. The more outrageous the claims, the more it would look like a fake story to everyone. Especially with the cartoon mugshot. It was probably best to skip the vampire angle, but if Audrey worked it out right, no one would take it seriously anyway. Rachel would have her revenge, but the whole thing would blow over as soon as Melicia posted her next review of some lame horror film. Maybe this could work.

"It's going up whether you help us or not," Rachel said.

"Fine," Audrey agreed. "Let's do it."

2

The blog went up.

CLARA BARTON CRIME LORD:
SCHOOL DEAN EXPOSED

Rachel thought it was the greatest thing ever.
But apparently no one else cared.

The post got a couple of likes but no comments. Two days went by, then three, and still no one at school had brought it up. It was as if the story had never been posted at all. Hope Barcomb marched through the halls of Clara Barton as she always did, making jokes and fart noises to her heart's content.

Audrey was honestly a little surprised.

They'd spent all weekend pulling the post together and it was pretty well done. She'd written that Dean Barcomb didn't have the background he said he did and added fake quotes from students who claimed to have paid Barcomb to get out of trouble. They'd even created and posted some fake documents. It was ridiculous.

Still, the fewer people who saw it, the better. Audrey had been pushing Bryant to finish his next *Pi Chronicles* cartoon so they could get another post up as soon as possible. And there was probably some new binge-worthy series that Melicia could write about. Audrey figured it was only a matter of time before the Barcomb post would be lost beneath all the newly posted articles.

On the fourth day, however, someone commented claiming he'd paid Dean Barcomb $100 to get out of trouble for trying to leave school grounds without a pass.

Then more comments started appearing: "not surprised" and "bet they didn't even check his resume."

Another: "This school will hire anyone! SMH."

The link popped up in a group chat Audrey was in. Then Dean Barcomb's picture—his *real* picture, not the cartoon one Bryant had drawn—showed up as a meme and made the rounds.

Audrey didn't say anything to Rachel, Mel, or Bryant, and they returned the favor. Usually they didn't talk much about old posts—it would be too easy to be overheard and caught.

But by the end of the week, even with Melicia's new movie review posted, people were talking about the Barcomb post all over the school. They all seemed to be wondering if it was true. Audrey couldn't tell if the story's comments were real or if others were just joining in on the joke. For her part, she mostly ignored the talk or laughed about how stupid it was.

When her dad asked how school was, like he did *every* night at dinner, she didn't bring up the gossip. Usually, she gave him a full report. It was just the two of them—her mom had left for good when she was little—and they had always been pretty open. But not about the blog. Not about this.

Still, Audrey was confident that all she and her friends needed to do was make it to the weekend. Gossip and stupid memes had short shelf lives. A day or two at most. One weekend would put an end to it, she was sure.

Mostly sure, anyway.

* * *

Audrey and her dad went to visit Audrey's grandma over the weekend. It was a good distraction. She didn't have to think about the blog. And she was glad to not have to face her three friends until this mess was all cleared up.

But by Monday, it had only gotten bigger.

Four more people had claimed online that they'd paid off Barcomb.

Another wrote Barcomb once "joked about having a degree in Poultry Science."

Hope Barcomb now walked down the hall to the sound of chickens clucking.

You could almost feel her anger, like something out of Greek mythology. The lockers practically shook as she passed. It was amazing but also awful.

"Nope, she clearly can't take a joke," Rachel beamed after school when they all gathered at Melicia's house.

"We should delete the post," Audrey argued. "Like, right now."

"Why?" Bryant asked, shrugging. "It's obviously fake. And it's working exactly the way we wanted it to. Did you see Hope today? Even her own friends are giving her a hard time."

"Good," Rachel said. "That's what she gets for having such lousy friends. Let her get a taste of her own medicine for a change."

"I agree with Audrey," Melicia said quietly. "It's probably good to take it down now."

"I thought you said no one could figure out who put it up," Bryant said, turning toward her with a frown.

"They can't," Melicia said. "But we don't want anyone looking too hard either. If it turns into a thing . . ." She trailed off.

"Like a legal thing." Audrey couldn't keep the edge out of her voice.

"Right. Maybe the cops could . . . I don't know." Melicia looked a little nervous. "They'll maybe figure it was loaded from the library and get security footage or something."

"Oh, please." Rachel waved off the idea. "No, they won't."

Bryant's voice was a little too high and strained. "I thought you used that special software stuff."

"I do, but," Melicia shrugged, "why mess around with it? Let's just delete it and be done. Audrey's right. Hope's been knocked down a peg. Let it go."

"I vote yes," Audrey said quickly. "Take it down."

"Me too." Melicia turned to Bryant. "I'm not even gonna ask dear Rachel."

Rachel grinned. "I think we should publically accuse her mother of witchcraft."

"Now who's the bully?" Audrey glared.

"It was a joke!" Rachel laughed. "Jeez, lighten up. Fine. We don't even need Bryant's vote. Take it down."

"Good," Audrey said, relief washing over her whole body.

"Who wants to go to the library with me?" Melicia asked. Her tech skills made her involvement almost mandatory. She was the only one who knew how to use the special flash drive she made with the software that messed with the coding to keep the posts anonymous. But it didn't seem right to make her go alone.

"I have a shift at the supermarket soon," Rachel said quickly.

Bryant shrugged. Audrey guessed that was a no.

"I'll go," Audrey said.

* * *

Audrey knew she was just being paranoid, but she felt like everybody at the library was watching them as Melicia logged into a computer. Her eyes darted from person to person—an older woman who lived a few houses away from Bryant, a girl she recognized from her math class, one of the kids she played soccer with when they were little—all of whom would be able to identify her.

The nerves that she had when they first started posting on the blog, nerves that had gone away after the first couple of months of making these regular trips to the library, were suddenly back. To cover her uneasiness, she started talking to Melicia a little too loudly about her English class. The librarian looked up from what he was doing at his computer, and a guy with a Clara Barton baseball T-shirt gave her an odd look. Audrey realized she was just calling more attention to herself and quickly shut up.

An hour later, the post and all the comments were deleted. As if they'd never been there. With the blog post gone, Audrey was sure the whole thing would finally blow over.

She was wrong.

3

The story was gaining momentum like a giant snowball. A snowball being pushed by about four hundred people.

Shortly before Audrey and Melicia took down their post, a student's parent had seen the blog and printed it off. That parent had gone to some other parents. And they had brought it to the school administration.

By the next day, the school was asking questions.

It wasn't long before Mr. Barcomb wasn't in school.

And on Friday, the local news ran the story.

First on their website and then on their morning broadcast:

LOCAL ADMINISTRATOR SUSPENDED

Audrey could hardly breathe. *No, no, NO.*

She was desperate to talk about it even though she knew it was risky. She grabbed Melicia outside of her AP Psych class.

"Did you hear—" Audrey started.

"Yes," Melicia stopped her, pulling Audrey down the hall. "Of course. Everyone's heard by now."

"He *actually* used a fake resume?" Audrey couldn't believe she was saying it aloud. It was shocking. Their fake story apparently had some truth to it.

Melicia breathed deeply. "Looks like it."

Audrey shivered. "Do you think they're going to fire him?"

"Who knows?" Melicia shrugged. "I probably read the same article you did. There was something about some certification he didn't finish. Some place he only subbed at a couple times but claimed he taught there."

"Yeah, like thirty years ago. Who cares?" Audrey was in full panic mode now. "We should tell someone."

Melicia frowned at her. "Tell them what, exactly, Audrey?"

"That the post was fake," Audrey said. "The documents. The bribery stuff. All of it."

"Well, I guess they found *something* that was real," Melicia said. "Enough to suspend him at least. I don't know."

"But whatever they found probably isn't nearly as bad as the stuff we made up. Not bad enough that he deserves to lose his job over it. God, I feel . . ."

"Terrible?" Melicia finished.

"Yes," Audrey admitted.

"Join the club."

"And the post is deleted. Like, *gone* gone, right?" Audrey needed to make sure. "No chance that the old post is saved on some computer somewhere or anything?"

"I can't promise that," Melicia said. "People could have taken screenshots of it.

But the whole site's down now if that makes you feel better."

Audrey's brows shot up. "You took down whole blog?"

"You bet I did," said Melicia. "They're going to come looking for us. For whoever made that post, that site. So it seemed best if there's no site at all."

"I guess."

"No emails about this," Melicia warned. "No texts either. This is . . . bad. Red alert stuff."

"I know," said Audrey.

"I'll talk with Rachel," Melicia promised. "Can you get Bryant?"

"Okay. Is Rachel . . . How is she? I've been looking for her all day."

"She's freaking out," Melicia admitted. "And I don't blame her. But let me deal with that. You just make sure Bryant stays quiet. I gotta go." Melicia stepped back into the current of students passing between classes. "Talk later." She vanished into the crowd.

Audrey was alone again in the hall. Alone but surrounded by a thousand classmates moving past her in every direction. They were all moving so fast. She felt like throwing up.

She rushed down the hall and burst into the bathroom and an open stall. Audrey stood frozen, perched over the toilet, trying to breath. Her whole body was shaking.

The bell rang.

What could she do to fix this? Maybe she could write another article, a *real* article, to help Mr. Barcomb get his side of the story out to the public. The news said the investigation was ongoing. Maybe there was a chance she could stop things from becoming any worse. She knew where Hope lived. She could go over there tonight, maybe even admit to what had happened. Try to explain.

But even as the thought crossed her mind, Audrey knew there was nothing she could do. As soon as she admitted that they'd made up all their accusations, she would be done. They all would. They'd be expelled or even arrested.

Melicia was right. They needed to keep quiet. Lay low until all of this was over. Even a snowball a hundred feet wide melts eventually.

Audrey flushed the empty toilet and walked back into the hall.

She was late to math class. She slunk toward her usual chair as quietly as possible, willing herself to become as small as she could so that Mr. Ward wouldn't notice her.

"Audrey, how nice of you to join us." Mr. Ward turned toward her. "An office runner dropped off a note."

Everyone watched Audrey grab the small light blue pass. Before she even got the chance to read it, she knew what it was—an infamous "CK Now" slip that would send her to the main office immediately. The most notorious pass in the whole school.

Carla Kramer. Principal.

NOW.

Audrey's heart lurched so hard she thought it would burst out of her chest, and all of the sudden she felt dizzy enough to faint.

The snowball just kept on rolling.

4

Principal Carla Kramer was actually Doctor
Carla Kramer, the PhD kind. Everyone assumed
she was super smart, and from everything
Audrey had heard, she was. Audrey hadn't ever
talked to her. As principal, Kramer mostly just
dealt with serious discipline problems, talked to
parents, and gave speeches at school functions.
All Audrey knew about her was that she drove
a Jaguar and always dressed nicely.

Audrey waited outside Kramer's office for
a good fifteen minutes. The whole time, the
office assistant at the front desk kept looking
over at her. And she did *not* like the faces he
was making.

Finally, the door opened and Kramer stepped out. "Sorry to keep you waiting, Audrey," she said, smiling. "Got stuck on an important phone call. Please, come in."

Audrey trudged into the office. The room was bigger than she had expected, with huge windows that overlooked neat rows of bushes and the entrance of the school.

"Have a seat," said Kramer, shutting the door and gesturing to one of two chairs in front of her desk.

Audrey took the first, wondering why it was so cold in the principal's office. Cold enough to make her shiver. *Stay calm*, she reminded herself. *And don't say anything.*

"How's your year going?" the principal asked, taking the other chair right beside her.

"Fine. Good," Audrey responded.

"Everyone always says junior year is the hardest," Kramer prodded.

"Yes, that's what I've heard too."

Kramer was a cat playing with its food. *Just get to it, already!* Audrey wanted to shout.

"Mrs. Raymond says you're probably going

to be our school paper's editor in chief next year. Is that right?" Kramer asked, clasping her hands together.

"Oh, I don't know," Audrey replied.

"You're the features editor this year, correct?"

"Yes, ma'am."

"You wrote the pieces on . . ." Kramer reached over to her desk and checked a small notepad covered in handwriting. "Homeless teens, and the one on teen dating violence. Both excellent, by the way."

"Thank you." Audrey could barely breathe.

"Oh," Kramer grinned. "And the one on teen 'foodies.' Fun one."

Audrey kept still.

Kramer asked, "I heard you've also written some for the local paper, *The Star*. Is that right?"

"Yes," Audrey answered. "I, um, was covering high school sporting events last year. They pay forty dollars an article."

"Very impressive," Principal Kramer said. "Your dad must be very proud. I assume you're thinking of journalism for college?"

"I don't know." The fact that Kramer brought up her dad made Audrey's heart beat a little faster.

"I hope so, Audrey. You've definitely got the talent for it."

Audrey blinked but said nothing. She couldn't get over how Kramer had worked in a mention of her dad. *Had Kramer already called him? Would she? Did he know his daughter was caught up in the town scandal?* Then, after she realized Dr. Kramer was still staring at her, waiting for a response. "Oh . . . Well, thank you."

"So, Audrey, what do *you* think of this whole Dean Barcomb mess?" Kramer asked.

Audrey tried very hard not to breathe too loudly. *Kramer doesn't know—she doesn't know!* Not for certain, anyway. She was just fishing for information. So Audrey simply shrugged. "I don't." No other words came. She hoped Kramer would just move on.

"Did you see the article in the local paper?" Kramer asked.

"No," she lied easily and quickly.

Principal Kramer nodded "What about that blog?"

Audrey held still. "The blog?"

"*The Espresso*—the 'unofficial news of Clara Barton High.' The not-so-secret blog everyone reads."

"No," she said. "I mean, I've read it a couple times—most kids have, but . . ."

"But?"

"I never saw anything about Mr. Barcomb on it."

Principal Kramer picked up the notepad and studied it before speaking again. "We think that's where all of this started," Kramer said.

Audrey nodded, trying to appear disappointed in someone. Someone who definitely wasn't her. "I thought the newspaper found—"

"Oh," Kramer shook her head. "I can't discuss that, but whatever the newspaper and the school may do, it's this blog that started things. I've read it a couple times. The whole site's recently been taken down, but we printed

29

copies of a handful of posts a few days ago. And you know what's funny?"

"What?"

"I think this Barcomb thing was maybe meant as a joke," the principal said. "There's a certain feel to it."

Audrey sat as still as possible. Hardly daring to breath.

"It seemed like it was going for over the top, as if it wasn't meant to be taken seriously. But then it got blown out of proportion. And now someone who's been a valued colleague of mine for years is under scrutiny because of it. Of course, if he's done anything shady, we need to know so the appropriate actions can be taken. But if this whole thing started with lies that made a mountain out of a molehill, we need to get to the bottom of that too."

Audrey said nothing.

"I suspect," Kramer went on, "the person, or persons, who ran that blog feel terrible about this whole thing. I'm not going to pretend there won't be consequences. But I'm doing my best to get out ahead of this thing before it becomes a legal matter. I've talked with the authorities and they've agreed to let this be a school issue if we can handle this *at* school. Do you understand?"

"Yes," Audrey managed to say.

"Good." The principal looked closely at Audrey. "So, while you're working on your next story for the paper, if you hear anything, or if there's anything you want to tell me, my door is always open. Got it?"

"Yes, ma'am." Audrey gulped. Her words sounded strangled, even to her. She was doomed. They were all doomed.

"Are you friends with Hope?" Kramer asked.

"Um, no, not really," Audrey stammered. "I mean, I know her, but I wouldn't say we're friends."

Principal Kramer nodded. "I know this has been hard on that whole family. I was just wondering if anyone had heard from her. Okay, then." She smiled broadly and stood. "We better get you back to class."

Audrey's legs were noodles, which made standing tough. Walking out of Kramer's office was practically a miracle. But she did it.

Not bad for a doomed person.

5

"She's bluffing," Rachel said as the friends all gathered at her house after school. Kramer had tried the same questioning routine with all of them. None of them had cracked. "She doesn't know anything."

"She knows." Audrey shook her head. The more she thought about it, the more she was sure. "Kramer *totally* knows. And even if she doesn't, we have to say something now. It's gone too far."

"It *has* gone too far," Melicia agreed. "But that's why we stay quiet. It's gotten way too big now. We'd be expelled. Maybe even arrested."

"I don't wanna go to jail." Bryant held up a hand as if he was voting.

"All we have to do is stick together and we're good," Melicia insisted. "This goes away in another week, tops. Seriously, there's no way she can prove it was us. The site's gone and I destroyed the flash drive. It would take, like, the FBI to trace things back to the library."

"I could probably do tattoos for my fellow inmates in prison," Bryant said reflectively.

"Look," Rachel said as she rubbed her forehead. "I know, I know. We messed up. *I* messed up. It was a bad idea, and I'm the one who put us in this—"

"We *all* did it," Audrey stopped her. "We all wanted to teach Hope a lesson. You're not taking the fall for something we did as a group."

"Let's just drop it," Melicia said. "Our blogging days are over anyway. At least for a *long* time."

"Okay," Rachel said, nodding in agreement. "Let's make a pact to never discuss it again." She held out her hand. "It never happened."

Rachel wiggled her outstretched hand, and Bryant put his hand in next to hers.

Audrey sat frozen. She didn't really want to make a pact. But how could she avoid it?

"I'm not making some secret pact," Melicia said. "That's corny. And kinda insulting. Everyone just stay quiet."

"Right. It never happened," Rachel said again. Audrey tried to avoid catching anyone else's eye as they all nodded.

* * *

It never happened. The words rolled around in Audrey's head all night.

It'd taken hours to finally fall asleep. Then she'd jerked awake in the middle of the night anyway, gasping for air as if waking from some nightmare she couldn't remember. Her heart thumping, she grabbed her phone and checked the time. It was two in the morning. She tossed the phone to the foot of her bed and stared up at the ceiling. *It never happened.*

But it wasn't true. Mr. Barcomb was suspended. Hope hadn't been back in school for days. And she and her friends were responsible for all of it.

She lay in the dark staring up at the ceiling. As if the answer was written there somewhere in the shadows above her bed. Nothing was there.

Not even when the sunlight appeared.

«

6

Five days later the basement was still nasty even after she'd been cleaning it all day. Sorting through the boxes packed with junk. Sweeping and dusting. Dragging things up the steps and out to the trash cans. And, when she was done with the basement, there was the whole fence in the backyard that needed a second coat of paint. Oh, and more yard work. Usually her dad didn't care too much about that kind of thing. But not now. Now he was actually *inventing* work to be done.

It was all part of Audrey's punishment for writing the blog post.

She'd come clean at school on Monday. Admitted everything to Principal Kramer.

Okay, not *everything*. She'd confessed to writing the blog post. But she said she'd done it all herself and that it had always been her blog. She accepted full responsibility and whatever punishment would come with it. If the others wanted to stay anonymous, that was their business and she could respect that. But she didn't have the guts for that, or maybe, she'd just finally decided that telling the truth was the right thing to do. Lies grew, after all.

Her dad was called into the school. He'd taken forever, it seemed, and then once he'd gotten there, all Audrey wanted was for him to disappear again. Her dad just kept shaking his head at her.

She'd kept it together until she saw the disappointment in his face. Then, Audrey had lost it and broken into tears. She had kept apologizing to him and Principal Kramer, and had tried to explain it had been a stupid joke.

During the crying, she was suspended.

Kramer used some generic violation in the

student handbook about social media behavior and school-related topics. It seemed like something they could argue if they wanted, but her dad wasn't in any mood to argue. And neither was Audrey.

Probation would follow when she got back. Including some service hours around the school. But she managed to dodge any legal charges. Back home, she'd also lost her laptop, car keys, and television privileges

Then the chores came. Her dad decided she'd be spending the entire two weeks of her suspension painting the fence, doing yard work, and cleaning the house. And she wasn't allowed headphones or the radio as a distraction while she worked.

Audrey supposed it was a small price for ruining someone's life. She actually thought she'd gotten off pretty easily.

But then the real price came. And Audrey hadn't seen it coming.

Melicia and Bryant were suspended too.

Despite Audrey's claims that she'd worked alone, Principal Kramer had called in all the others again one at a time. Everyone at school knew the four of them were good friends. Kramer had explained to them that Audrey had admitted to writing the blog and then had given them each a second chance to admit *their* involvement. Two had.

Only Rachel, it seemed, had stuck to the plan. She was still at school. Or at least Audrey assumed she was. All of her friends were ignoring her texts. She tried to tell herself it was because they'd lost their phones as punishment, but Rachel hadn't gotten in trouble yet and Audrey had tried texting one of Melicia's burner phones that her parent's didn't know about.

Eventually, she had gotten so desperate that she grabbed her dad's phone when he had gone off to take a shower. She figured her friends might be more likely to answer if they didn't recognize her number. But when she called Melicia, it had been awful. Melicia finally answered, but Audrey had only gotten out a word or two before Melicia hung up. Audrey couldn't believe it. Melicia wouldn't even hear her out. It might have been better if Melicia had yelled at her. Ever since they first became friends, Audrey had been able to talk to Melicia—even when they were angry with each other. But not now.

She had no doubts Bryant and Rachel were furious with her too.

She'd gone against the plan. How could she ever look them in the eye again? She imagined ways of defending her decision. But her explanations always fell short. She'd spent all day second-guessing her choice to talk to Kramer. *Why, why, why?* It'd been so stupid.

Audrey choked back a sob then got back to work.

When she was done, she slowly climbed back upstairs. She felt like a ghost moving through her own house, drifting from place to place. Her friends and family were all disgusted with her. And they should be.

Audrey collapsed onto her bed. All she wanted to do was sleep. She curled up, grabbed one of her pillows, and hugged it tightly. She tried imagining what things would be like in a week, a month, a year. Eventually this feeling would pass. It had to.

She reached out for her phone to check the time and saw there was a new message.

Audrey was thrilled. It had to be one of the others finally reaching out. Maybe it was Melicia texting to apologize for hanging up on her.

Reply yes for a free do-over

Audrey squinted at the single sentence, confused. A chill ran up her back.

None of her friends' names was connected to the text. It's been sent from someone *not* in her contacts.

Weird.

Maybe Melicia had sent it from a burner phone Audrey didn't know about.

She checked the information on the message and it wasn't connected to any name *or* number. There was nothing. It was as if the message had come from nowhere and no one.

Whoever had sent it, Audrey knew she

had to do something to start putting their friendship back together. If the others wanted to keep on hating her, that was their choice. But she had to start trying to make things right.

Audrey's dad was out for the whole day, and she was due for a lunch break anyway. It was a perfect time for a quick escape.

She jumped out of bed. Bryant's house was the closest—barely three blocks. They'd been friends since kindergarten. If she couldn't fix *that* relationship, she didn't stand a chance with the other two.

She found him sitting out front on his porch.

"Hey," she managed.

Bryant looked up. "Hey." His voice was unusually soft.

"Um, what's up?" she asked.

"Well, my dad's coming home from work early to take me out to some guy's farm. Literally to start painting this dude's barn. Says it'll be a better use of my artistic talents." Bryant added air quotes around the last bit. "But I suppose maybe I do deserve it."

Audrey could hardly breathe. She wanted

him to yell or mock her or threaten her with angry bees. "Bryant." His name was all she could get out

"What?" He looked away. "What do you want me to say?"

"I'm sorry. I didn't . . ."

He shrugged, looked back at her. "Dude, it is what it is."

"I *never* mentioned you guys," she said, desperate for him to know that.

"I know," Bryant said. "Principal Kramer was clear about that. And honestly, I never thought you did."

Audrey felt the tears well up behind her eyes, and she fought to keep her voice steady. She struggled for the next words. "I thought it was the best thing to do."

"Well," he looked away again, his voice more strained, "maybe you're right. But at this point it doesn't matter. We serve our suspension time and move on. Of course, everyone knows which three students are missing from class. And Hope Barcomb only ran with the most popular kids in the school.

The rest of this year, and next, should be a super thrill. But, if that's what we get for ruining some dude's life then, like I said, maybe you were right."

"Have you seen Rachel?" she asked.

"No. She's not talking to us." He shrugged at Audrey's stare. "She's afraid of getting caught too," he said. "Or—"

"Or maybe she's too embarrassed for *not* also turning herself in," Audrey said.

"Yup, or that." He pushed some hair from his face. "Probably that."

"What about Melicia?" Audrey asked. "Have you talked with her?"

He nodded. "She's mad, Audrey."

"I know," Audrey said. "But that's why I wanted to—"

"*I'm* mad," he added, cutting her off. "When you went to Kramer, you kinda took away all our options. Once she had you, getting the rest of us was too easy. She knew we were friends."

Audrey's world narrowed to a pinprick. "Were?"

"Whatever. Let's not focus too much on word choice here. You should have said something—warned us before you caved. We could have discussed it. The four of us have had a democracy on everything since the seventh grade. What movie to watch. Which of my cartoons to post. Where to meet for coffee." He gave her a weak smile. "You picked a heck of a time to go out on your own."

Audrey swallowed. Her heart felt way too big for her chest, thick and hot. Her throat felt like it had started to close up. *What had she done?* "Does she hate me?" she barely whispered.

"She's mad, yeah. But let's not get too dramatic. Like I said, move on. Just let some time pass."

"How much time? A week? A year?" She asked.

"Audrey . . ." Bryant looked away.

"Do *you* hate me?" Audrey asked.

"Just let some time pass," he said again.

* * *

Audrey stumbled home. It felt like it took weeks.

She still had to paint half the fence outside, but she didn't care anymore.

Audrey dragged herself to her bedroom, shut the door, and collapsed onto her bed. Everyone she cared about was against her now. Her friends, her dad, her teachers. Even, she admitted, herself.

She'd never felt so alone in her whole life.

She looked at her cell phone.

Reply yes for a free do-over

Audrey bit her lip as she typed a reply.

She wrote just one word then turned the phone off.

《《

7

Audrey woke the next morning to the familiar tune of her phone alarm.

It was 6:10 a.m. *What the heck?* She knew she'd turned it off. There was no point in setting the alarm so early when she didn't have school.

She rolled over and almost landed on her laptop. Audrey jerked up in her bed.

How did her laptop get there? She had been known to fall asleep while watching shows, but she hadn't seen her laptop since Monday when her dad took it away. She looked around and spotted her car keys on her desk.

It looked like her dad had ended the punishments during the night. *But why would he do that?* Audrey wondered. There was no way he was *that* impressed with her work on the basement and the fence. She was glad he was starting to ease up, but she couldn't understand why.

She set the phone back down and closed her eyes again. The rest of the day, the rest of her life, could wait. Melicia and Bryant still hated her—that could definitely wait. She'd finish painting the fence *after* her dad went off to work. Until then, she'd just continue to hide in her room. She kinda thought he preferred it that way, too.

Then, a half hour later, there was a rap at her door.

"Audrey?" It was her dad. "You up?"

Audrey scowled at the door. *Guess the punishments aren't ending after all.* He wanted her back to work ASAP. "Yeah," she said. "I'll be right out." She dressed for painting, an old t-shirt and her worst jeans, and went downstairs.

Her father was getting ready for the day. It was the usual routine she'd seen a thousand times. "There's a look." He grimaced, then smiled over his coffee. "You really *are* running late today."

Audrey moved quietly into the kitchen. She thought she'd grab a bowl of cereal and use the time to gauge her dad's mood. Getting her laptop and car keys back were a definite step in the right direction. If she could achieve peace at home, that'd be a great start. Next, no matter how hard it was, she'd focus on her friends. Then eventually, maybe, she could even make amends with the Barcombs. Somehow.

There were two brown bags on the counter. Most days, her dad was up before six and made lunch for both of them. In return, she usually took care of their dinners. Her dad winked. "We both get egg salad for today."

Audrey stared at the two bags.

"What's wrong?" he asked. "You love egg salad."

"Yeah, I do," Audrey said, confused. "Where—where are we going?"

Her dad laughed. "You better grab something for breakfast fast. You have another five minutes before traffic gets really bad, and then you'll be late to school again. And I don't want to be called down to see the principal."

Audrey felt like the whole room was spinning. "But . . ."

"You okay?" her dad asked. Then, before she had a chance to answer, he added, "Hurry up!" He left her alone in the kitchen.

She moved to the window and looked outside. The backyard fence was faded, and in need of a good paint job.

She grabbed hold of the sink.

"Audrey!" Her dad called.

"I'm going!" she called, but instead of heading toward the door she turned down the hall to the basement door. She opened it slowly like she was opening an old crypt. Terrified of what was lurking just behind.

She flicked on the light and looked down the steps.

The basement was a disaster. It was dusty and cluttered with paint cans and old empty boxes everywhere. It looked as if no one had cleaned it in years. Had her dad gone down in the middle of the night and made it dirty again or—

Reply yes for a free do-over.

Audrey pulled out her phone and looked at her texts.

The message was gone, along with the reply she'd sent

Yes.

Her most recent text had come from Melicia on Thursday night.

She opened her internet app and went to her favorites.

The blog appeared. It was back up!

But not the Dean Barcomb post. The last post was one of Mel's movie reviews.

She checked her phone calendar for the date. It was Friday.

Last Friday!

No, that's impossible. How could it be? Audrey thought to herself.

Had the last week just been some nightmare, or was she in a nightmare now? Either way, it made no sense. This was crazy.

Audrey blew out a long breath. She had to figure out what was going on. Focus on the facts.

Facts: The blog was up and active again. She had her laptop and keys back. Her dad was yelling at her to go to school, and he was in a good mood. The date on her phone said it was the previous Friday. The fence wasn't painted. The basement wasn't clean.

With trembling fingers, she pulled up her internet app again and typed in Barcomb's name and the school. Then blinked.

Facts: The news article was still there. Dean Barcomb had been suspended. The investigation was ongoing.

This wasn't some magical "do-over." Nothing had changed at all!

Well, nothing but the fence and basement and the rest of her punishments. It made no sense.

Audrey buried her whole face in her hands, trying to work it out.

"You're going to be late!" her dad shouted again from upstairs.

Audrey screamed into her hands, then ran back to her room for her car keys and her backpack. Maybe there would be more answers at school. Maybe something would make sense. Or maybe this was all a silly dream and she'd wake up on the way there.

She didn't.

8

The rest of day was just as confusing.

It was *déjà vu* to the extreme.

Every class, every person she saw, she'd seen it all before. She was reliving the exact same moments. But she didn't take part in the events moving around her. She'd become only an observer.

Melicia, Bryant, and Rachel were all also back in school. And they were all talking to her again. The gossip going around was still about Hope and Mr. Barcomb. She was even called down to Principal Kramer's office where she talked to the principal. The questions were all the same, but Audrey wasn't taken by surprise by Kramer's tactics this time. Mostly she just shrugged and said. "No, ma'am."

After school, they all ended up at Rachel's again, talking about what to do. Just like before. The same exact talk, except her voice was now out of it. She kept her words to herself. It was strange enough hearing everyone else's words again.

"Look," Rachel said again. "I know, I know. We messed up. *I* messed up. It was a bad idea, and I'm the one who put us in this. So let me help get us out."

Silence. This was the part where Audrey had insisted that they stick together—that it was all of their plans. But now, she couldn't help feeling a little bitter about how Rachel was the only one who didn't get in trouble when she came clean.

Audrey didn't say anything.

"Let's just drop it," Mel chimed in. "Our blogging days are over anyway. At least for a *long*, long time."

"Okay. Let's make a pact to never discuss it

again," Rachel said, nodding and holding out her hand.

"It never happened," Audrey blurted out.

Melicia laughed. "Exactly."

Rachel wiggled her outstretched hand. Bryant put his hand in. Then Mel.

Audrey put her hand over all of theirs. "It never happened," she said again, more to herself than to the others. After all, how else could she explain today?

That night, Audrey retreated to her room after dinner to "do homework" just like she had before, but she just sat for hours curled in her bed, trying to work it all out in her head. She knew she had the power to act differently than the first time she'd lived this same day. But did she fix things enough to avoid ruining her friendships? Audrey had already altered the scene at Rachel's house. They'd sworn to keep quiet together now. *She'd* sworn.

She hoped she had done enough this time.

* * *

Monday morning, she didn't go in to see Principal Kramer.

She kept her promise. She admitted nothing.

No fence to paint. No suspension. She and her friends played old board games all night and talked about all sorts of things but never once brought up the Barcomb stuff.

It never happened.

9

Audrey was in the cafeteria with Rachel, who was grinning.

"What are you so happy about?" Audrey asked.

Rachel stabbed a finger at a passing teacher. "I'm thinking about Mrs. Kindt."

Audrey watched Mrs. Kindt pass by on her way to talk to some other teachers. "Why's that?"

"Wondering what other injustices we should bring out into the world," Rachel said. "All her political rants in class are starting to get to me. Isn't it supposed to be an AP Psych class?"

Audrey frowned. "I'll pass, thanks. You know, we didn't bring any injustice out. We just hurt someone."

"Nope, not true," Rachel countered. "Barcomb had actually forged his resume."

"That's still being investigated," Audrey corrected. "And we're not discussing this, remember? You said so yourself."

"Right, right. Still . . ." Rachel was clearly still thinking about the next person they could go after with the blog.

"No. And, seriously, stop talking about it." Audrey looked around. "Someone *will* hear you."

"Oh, please," Rachel waved the concern away with her hand. "Calm down. No one's listening to us. You can't hear a thing in this zoo."

Audrey looked around anyway. They were sitting by a table with some other junior girls that were all talking about their history assignment, a table of baseball players joking around with each other, and a table full of seniors where one of the guys seemed to be doing a cruel but accurate impression of the gym teacher. Nobody seemed to be paying any attention to them, but Audrey returned to her lunch and changed the subject. "You do the reading for English? Heard there's a quiz."

"I found a summary online," Rachel said through a very full bite of her sandwich.

"Well, that's more than you usually do," Audrey said, smiling.

Rachel winked. "So how about we start checking into Will and Evan Stecz? Everyone knows what's going on with—"

"No!" Audrey slammed her hand down on the table. This time a few people from the surrounding tables *did* look around.

Rachel was clearly shocked. "Woo, girl. Take it easy. I didn't realize you were in charge of *everything* now."

"I'm not," said Audrey. "But there isn't even a blog anymore. We're not going to post anything. I don't understand why you keep talking about this."

"Hey, Audrey?" It was another voice behind

her and she turned. It was one of the office runners. He was holding a blue pass.

Oh no, not again.

"CK wants to see you now," he said.

Audrey didn't have to wait this time.

She was led right into Principal Kramer's office.

"Just wanted to follow up on the whole Barcomb blog-post situation," Kramer said. She remained standing as Audrey sat down. "The school's been working with the police, tracking some things. I spoke with Melicia Jones. She's a friend of yours, right? I heard she was some kind of a computer expert?"

"Sure, I guess so," Audrey stuttered. She was thrown off by such a forward attack.

"You 'guess so'? Is she?"

"Well, yeah. I mean, I don't really know much about computers," Audrey said.

"I understand." Kramer loomed over Audrey like a hungry vulture. "Last time we spoke you said you'd try to look into things. All confidential, of course."

"No, I . . ." Audrey sat straighter. "You'd

suggested that if I heard anything, I could come to you." She shrugged. "But I haven't heard anything."

"Nothing?" Kramer raised her eyebrow.

"No," claimed Audrey. "Third quarter is wrapping up. I don't have time to do much more than my schoolwork right now."

Kramer—the vulture—clasped her hands in front of her chest. "You don't know anything about this, Audrey? Anything at all?"

"Sorry." Audrey sat back. "No, ma'am, I don't."

Kramer sighed, clearly frustrated. "Okay, then. Thanks for coming in to talk with me."

Audrey stood to leave. "Sure."

"Would you do me a favor?" Kramer passed her another blue slip. "Could you get this to Rachel Hodge?"

Audrey looked down at the slip. She realized her hand was shaking.

"I believe you two have the same lunch and usually sit together?"

Audrey tried to steady herself. "Yes, ma'am," she managed.

"Thanks," Kramer said.

Audrey could feel the vulture's eyes on her back the whole way out of the office and down the hall. When she was safely around the corner, she ran.

10

Audrey's friends waited for her while she had her school paper meeting after school—all three of them. A full-on ambush. They'd stopped her outside as she walked to her car.

"Hey!" Audrey said, forcing a smile. "What are you all doing here so late?"

"You wouldn't respond to our texts," replied Melicia as Rachel held up her own phone.

"Okay, sorry." Audrey made a *so what?* face. "I've been swamped all day. Haven't even looked at my phone. What's going on?"

"You tell us," Rachel said.

Audrey re-slung her schoolbag over to the other shoulder. "What is this?"

"What did you tell Kramer?" Melicia asked.

"Kramer?" Audrey's face scrunched into a tight, angry ball. "Nothing. Just like we said."

Rachel cut her off. "Kramer claims you were 'looking into this.' Maybe going to write a story or something."

"Oh, please." Audrey frowned. "She's so pathetic. Is that what she told you?"

"It's what she told him," Melicia nodded her head at Bryant. Bryant looked away.

"So what?" Audrey said. "I'm not writing any story. I told Kramer I didn't know anything. She keeps acting like I'm out gathering information on all of this or something."

"Are you?" Rachel asked, taking a weird sort of half step forward, almost menacing.

"Are you crazy?" Audrey snapped back. "Gathering info on what? On us? I told her I didn't know anything. End of story." Anger rumbled in her gut. "What'd *you* tell her, Rachel? You were in there an awfully long time at lunch."

"Don't even." Rachel crossed her arms and

looked away. "I'm the one who wanted to keep blogging, remember. I'm not the one who's freaking out."

"Well, blogging again *is* a horrible idea," Melicia said.

"So you're taking her side now?" Rachel snapped.

"I'm not taking anyone's side," Melicia said and shot Rachel a look. "So how about you bring it down some."

"Jeez, guys," Bryant laughed nervously. It wasn't a good sound. "How about *everyone* relax?"

Rachel spun on him. "Yeah? 'Relax'? You're the one she's gonna get first. All your drawings look exactly the same."

"Easy now . . ." Bryant held up his hands. "One, they don't. Two, I didn't say anything to anyone at school and won't. And, three—"

"Stop it!" Audrey yelled a little louder than she had intended. All three of her friends looked at her, a little startled. "Listen to us. I thought this was over. We put it behind us, blah, blah, blah."

"Well, Kramer does know we're all friends," said Melicia.

"And she'll put it all together," Rachel said. "The four of us having something to do with it. She clearly already suspects us."

Bryant shook his head, looking genuinely angry for the first time. "You said it was foolproof, Mel. You said we were safe."

"We are." Melicia shook her head. "Everything's fine."

"Right, it's all fine. Which is why you ambushed me," Audrey said sarcastically. Then, for good measure, she added, "But if you're so concerned about Kramer, why are you talking to me here in front of the school? Her office is right there." Audrey nodded back to the front of the school. "And there are cameras everywhere. They can see us, you know."

Her friends looked back at the school, a combination of realization and panic on their faces.

"What the . . . ? Seriously?!" Audrey tossed her head back and laughed, even *she* was startled by how mean the sound was. "Look at you! I was joking. Who cares if we're talking? Seriously, come on. When did everyone get so paranoid? I thought we were good."

"We're good," said Rachel. "We were making sure *you* are."

Audrey narrowed her eyes. "Yeah, I'm good. And I'll try to get over the fact that the three of you don't trust me."

"That's not true," said Bryant.

Audrey turned to him. "You know it is. Thanks a lot, dear friends."

"Hey, Audrey," Melicia reached out and gently grabbed her arm. "Look, we didn't mean anything by it. We just—"

"I gotta go." Audrey opened her car door. "See you later."

Audrey plopped down in her seat and started the car. Her three friends walked away together.

The car was still parked, and she gripped the steering wheel to stop her hands from shaking.

"Everything is okay," she said to herself out loud.

But that had been another lie. *I'm just tired,* she thought.

And angry. And hurt. And confused.

Audrey's phone buzzed. A message. She sighed and dragged the phone from her backpack.

No name again. But there was a number this time.

Still, Audrey didn't recognize it.

She opened the message anyway. And then gasped.

I know you wrote it. Was it fun to mess with someone's life like that? Hope so . . .

11

Audrey almost deleted the message about fifty times to get it off her phone and out of her mind forever. But she couldn't bring herself to actually do it. Not until she learned who sent it.

But no matter what she tried, she couldn't figure out where the text came from. This one wasn't like the do-over message. That message didn't seem to come from any number at all. *This* one came from a real number, but she couldn't figure out who it belonged to. She'd gone online to search the number but nothing came up. She'd even checked the school bulletin boards that no one used except over-eager club leaders. The phone number was nowhere to be found.

She thought about texting back but didn't want to encourage whoever this was. If she just ignored it, maybe the message—and whoever had sent it—would simply go away.

It never happened.

School was a nightmare. Audrey kept looking at classmates, trying to figure out which one had sent her the text. The idea that one of her own friends had sent it was not completely out of the question, which was a horrible thought. But the fact her three friends were all avoiding her, and one another, didn't help. Rachel skipped lunch. Bryant and Melicia, she noticed, walked solo down the halls. It looked like everyone was afraid that either Kramer or someone else at the school would see the four of them together and figure things out.

As the day went on, Audrey knew she couldn't keep living like this. So she texted Rachel, Mel, and Bryant.

Mel's house after school? Have news and
data issue.

They gathered there at 3:30. At least, most
of them did.

"Is Rachel coming?" Audrey asked.

Melicia shrugged. "She didn't say anything
to me. In fact she's ignored all of my texts
lately."

Bryant asked: "What's this big news?"

Audrey handed over her phone.

Bryant read the text and frowned. He
passed the phone on to Melicia. "Did you
check the number already?"

"Yeah. There's nothing," Audrey replied

"Mind if I try?" Melicia unlocked her
laptop and started typing. Audrey shook her
head, but Melicia wasn't looking at her anyway.

"Did either one of you get a text like this?"
Audrey asked nervously.

"No," Bryant said, and Melicia shook
her head.

"So why me?" asked Audrey.

"I thought the text was pretty clear about

that," Melicia replied. "You wrote the post."

"Well, yeah," Audrey snapped, feeling unreasonably stung. "With help. It's not like I randomly came up with this idea on my own."

Melicia kept her eyes glued to the screen. "In any case, it's a burner phone. Completely untraceable—some pre-paid disposable thing bought with cash. I can't tell who it's connected to."

"Um, don't . . ." Audrey started. "Don't *you* have a burner phone?"

Melicia looked up, her eyes narrowed. "Yeah. I have two, actually. And?"

"I don't know," Audrey said "I just . . . Are you sure there's no way to figure out who—"

"You think *I* sent this message?" Melicia asked.

Audrey shrank back. "No, I—No, that's not what I meant. I mean—*Did* someone here send the message?"

"What the heck?" Bryant stared in shock. "Are you being serious?"

"Well, you guys were in my face yesterday two minutes before I got this text. And where's Rachel? Why didn't she show up?"

"There," Mel said, shoving the phone back into Audrey's hands. "Sent."

Audrey's felt her stomach drop. "Sent?" She looked down on her phone. Melicia had texted back.

COWARD! WHO IS THIS?

"Oh my God!" Audrey gasped. "What did you do?"

"I sent a reply to your mysterious friend." Melicia opened up her desk drawer and pulled out a phone, then tossed it onto her bed. She pulled another from her backpack and then the smartphone from her front pocket, and she placed them beside the first. All three phones lay in a little pile, silent and dark. "Go ahead," she said. "Check 'em."

"Mel, I didn't mean—" Audrey couldn't move.

"No, please." Melicia waved her hand over

the phones. "Have at it. If I sent the original text, I'd get your response. Right?" There was a knock at the bedroom door. Melicia opened her door.

"Where have you been?" she growled at the newcomer.

"I was at work. Why? What's going on?" Rachel asked, stepping into the room.

"Our *friend* thinks we're sending her nasty messages," Melicia explained.

"That's not what I said," Audrey protested.

Bryant cut her off. "Show Rachel," he said.

Audrey handed over the phone. "I got this yesterday, but I never said that one of you sent it." She glared at Melicia.

"So what?" Rachel handed the phone back. "It's Kramer or Hope or anyone else. Seriously, who cares? No one knows it's us, right? Or at least no one can prove it was."

"Have you guys said anything to anyone?" Bryant asked.

"What do you mean?" Rachel glared at him. "Why? Have *you*?"

"What? No," he responded, startled.

Audrey glared at the whole room. "I haven't said anything."

"You check the phones yet?" Melicia asked, turning her attention back to Audrey.

"I don't need to, Mel." At this point Audrey just wanted to get out of the room. A room of her closest friends who now felt like enemies. "I didn't mean to imply it was you."

Melicia stepped toward her. "Here, I'll do it for you." She opened up the first phone, turned it on, and shoved it at Audrey. "Nothing." She did it two more times. "Satisfied?"

Audrey stared at Mel. She couldn't decide if this version of events where Melicia was yelling at her was better or worse than the version where they weren't speaking at all.

"Are those *all* the phones you have?" Bryant asked.

Mel's eyes flashed at him, her mouth tightening. "Get out of my house."

"Guys . . ." Audrey could barely get out the single word.

"Fine." Bryant had grabbed his backpack. "Good luck, all."

"Did you tell anyone, Goodluck boy?" Rachel asked him again.

"Who's *he* gonna tell?" Melicia snarked.

"So true," Rachel smiled meanly.

"I already said no," Bryant said.

"What about your stupid little brother?" Rachel challenged. "This texting crap sounds exactly like something he might pull."

"I haven't told anyone," he said. "Just like I promised my *friends*."

Rachel clapped slowly.

"Have a nice life," Bryant said and stepped out of the room.

Audrey started after him. "Bryant!" She turned. "Mel?"

"What?" Mel glared. "I have to stand here while all my friends accuse me?"

Rachel held up her hand. "I haven't said anything to you, so maybe chill out a bit."

Melicia eyed Rachel, deciding something. "I heard you were down in Kramer's office again," she said.

"So?" Rachel smirked. "We've all been down there."

"No, this was today. Someone saw you and asked me if I knew anything about it. A *third* visit?"

Rachel held out her hands. "And? What are you saying?"

"Why didn't you tell us?" Melicia was on the hunt now.

"It had nothing to do with this. Not everything involves Audrey's dumb article, you know."

"You seem pretty on edge considering I was just asking you a question," Melicia said.

Rachel shook her head as she looked between Melicia and Audrey. Her eyes were flat and dull. "We done here?"

"Definitely," Melicia said.

Yes, Audrey thought to herself. *That's exactly the word for us.*

Done.

《《

12

Audrey didn't want to go straight home after the blowup at Melicia's house. She didn't want her dad asking too many questions. So she decided to grab a smoothie at the strip mall on her way home. She hoped some time and the drink might help. But that was not the case.

As she walked past a Mexican restaurant she couldn't help but see the Barcombs, eating dinner at the table right by the front window. Dean Barcomb was sitting next to Hope with Hope's mom on his other side. Also at the table was a boy Audrey guessed was maybe eleven, a little girl who was probably nine-ish, and an older guy, probably seventy, who looked like an older Mr. Barcomb—his dad, Audrey assumed.

She stumbled, her body and mind in total disagreement about whether she should keep going forward or stay there looking at the Barcombs. What if one of them looked up and noticed her? She didn't think she could bear the idea of looking Hope or Dean Barcomb in the eye.

Still, she was frozen, staring like a deer in the headlights into the window of the Mexican restaurant.

She realized this was something she wouldn't have had to deal with if she hadn't taken the do-over. She never would have seen the Barcombs all sitting together like this if she was at home, grounded for admitting the truth. No, she was out and free. And the Barcombs were miserable.

No one at the table was talking or smiling. They were all just eating. The Barcomb family looked broken, actually. Hope looked deflated. Audrey thought back to the Hope who had made farting noises at Rachel as she passed.

The girl in the window now was completely different. Audrey couldn't even imagine her making a peep in the hallways at school.

Audrey jumped.

Hope's little sister was staring out the window at her. *Directly* at her. Their eyes locked. Audrey tried imagining the conversations this girl had heard in her house over the last two weeks. The whole town knew about this scandal now. Audrey wondered how much had filtered down to the elementary schools.

The girl turned her head, puzzled. Seeing something in Audrey's face she couldn't quite work out.

The whole family dinner scene blurred as Audrey's eyes welled up with tears again.

Audrey turned and ran back to her car.

She hid in her room the rest of the night. At one point, she thought of reaching out to her friends but couldn't bring herself to do it. There was radio silence from Rachel, Bryant, and Melicia. Maybe they were mad she'd accused them. Or blamed her for writing the post. Or for even thinking of it in the first place. Joke or not.

At midnight, her phone buzzed with a message.

She picked it up slowly, praying it would be one of her friends but knowing in her gut it wasn't. She knew exactly who'd sent it before she even looked. And she was right.

It was from the same sender that Melicia had texted back earlier.

Soon EVERYONE learns the truth. Unless . . .

‹‹

13

The truth.

What did that even mean anymore?

The truth was that she'd been living in some crazy alternative reality for the past two weeks. The truth was that her best friends all hated her. The truth was that she hated them back a little too.

The truth was that she no longer trusted them. Or anyone, really.

But she couldn't erase what had happened. She picked up her phone and reread the latest message.

Soon EVERYONE learns the truth. Unless . . .

What did soon mean? It could be hours or weeks. *Unless what?*

* * *

Audrey couldn't sleep, she couldn't pay attention in class or at paper meetings, and she spoke to her dad in cavewoman-ish grunts.

She'd never used her talent with words to hurt anyone before. And the fact that she'd done so "for her friends" didn't justify anything anymore. It only, strangely, made it worse. Their little blog had once been a worthy thing. It had grown to become exactly what they hoped it would be—a voice for the students. They got replies and feedback all the time from readers, but now the site was shut down. All the credibility they'd built, every opportunity they had, was gone.

Well, as of today, she was officially done with wasted opportunities. She grabbed her car keys and drove to the supermarket.

When Rachel finally saw Audrey, her face looked puzzled for a second before she looked away to return to her work. It was lucky for

Audrey that Rachel usually worked as a cashier on the weekends. This conversation needed to be face to face, and Rachel couldn't run away if Audrey caught her at work. Audrey stood in line, three people back. Waiting. Eventually, she was up.

"What are you doing here?" Rachel asked, swiping through the random assortment of candy Audrey had grabbed while waiting in line.

"I wanted to make sure you were okay," Audrey said.

Rachel rolled her eyes. "How nice. Buying anything else?"

Audrey grabbed another pack of gum and laid it on the belt. "So, are you okay?" she asked.

Rachel scanned the new items, but didn't respond.

"Well, I just wanted to tell you that if you needed anything, or anyone to talk to, know that . . . I hope you can still talk to me. I know you're probably mad at me. Or don't trust me or whatever. But you're one of my best friends."

Rachel started to argue but Audrey held up a hand to stop her. "You can yell at me later. I just wanted to say I'm here. And, also, that I'm really sorry."

"For what?" Rachel sighed. "We all did it." She looked back at the line growing behind Audrey. "I really need to get back to work."

"Sure, I understand," Audrey said. "Sorry to—"

"Eleven forty." Rachel gave the total cost of the all the junk Audrey had laid on the belt. Her face softened. "Do you really want all this?"

"No." Audrey handed her a twenty. "But maybe someday I'll be able to share some of it with Mel or something."

"Yeah," Rachel smiled sadly. "Hey, listen, Audrey—"

"We'll talk later," Audrey said, smiled back, and then took her change.

"Sure," Rachel agreed, but Audrey could tell neither one of them fully believed this.

After she left the supermarket she swung by Bryant's house to apologize to him too.

And then she made her way to the coffee shop where she knew Melicia sometimes hung out on the weekend. She didn't expect anything from them, but she knew she needed to at least make the effort.

It wasn't perfect. But it was a start.

As she pulled back up in front of her home, Audrey felt her phone buzz in her pocket. She waited until she was safely in her room before checking the message.

Today was all about her dealing with the fallout from her decisions over the last few weeks. And here, on her phone, was more fallout.

Library tonight at 10:00. Bring $200.

◀◀

14

Audrey got there at 9:30.

She knew the library closed at 9:00 and wanted to arrive after the last workers had left but before 10:00.

By 9:40, the parking lot was already completely empty except for her.

She sat alone in the car, waiting. She was tense, constantly shifting in her seat and looking around at the slightest sound or movement. Every minute felt like an hour.

Audrey had brought the $200 as told. Birthday gifts and money she made by writing for the local paper. Turned into hush money. Exactly what she deserved. Whether that would turn into weekly payments or stay a one-time thing, she didn't know. There were a dozen options on how this might play out. But unless one of the options included going back in time *again* and having never done the post in the first place—which didn't seem likely—none of her choices looked good.

At 10:00, a car pulled into the library lot. It circled around behind her car and then parked across the parking lot. She couldn't see the driver through the bright headlights blazing directly in her face. Then the headlights went dark.

The driver was sitting with a sweatshirt hood over their head, his or her face lost in the shadows. Then the driver got out of the car.

Her heart pounding way too loudly, Audrey stepped out too.

It was a guy. He moved in front of his car and then slid onto its hood. "I won't get any closer," he promised. "I didn't think through how scary this part would be for you."

Audrey was shaking, but somehow kept her voice steady. Mostly.

"Who are you?" she demanded.

He pulled back the hood on his Clara Barton baseball hoodie.

It was the guy who had looked at her funny when she and Melicia had gone to the library to take down the blog post. She recognized his face from school but couldn't remember his name.

"Nick Schaeffer," he said. "I'm the one who sent you the messages."

"I figured that part out," she said. "What do you want?"

"I asked you here because I wanted to apologize in person," he paused. "This was a *horrible* idea."

"Wait." Audrey blinked, then crossed her arms over her chest protectively. "What are you saying?"

"I wanted to teach you a lesson or something," Nick said. "All of you. And it went too far. This, this here, is nuts. If you wanna call the police on me or something, I don't blame you."

Wait, what? "I'm not going to call

the police," she said. She stepped closer. "Why me?"

"I don't know." Nick shrugged. "I was going to mess with Bryant first, but . . . I mean, you wrote the original article. That was easy to tell."

Despite herself, Audrey edged a little closer still. "How did you know?"

"I've read your articles in the school paper and a couple of the ones you wrote about my baseball games last year. You have a pretty distinct style. Plus . . . I've seen the four of you here. I mean at the library. I literally watched you and Melicia take down the post."

"You were spying on us?" Audrey said.

He laughed, and the sound wasn't creepy at all. "Don't flatter yourself. I was doing homework. I come here all the time, and I've seen you guys here before. I kept meaning to come over and say hi to you all sometime, but you're always pretty focused. That's how a lot of people are at the library. I like that it's quiet here but still has lots of people, you know."

"Yes," she agreed. "I do."

"Anyway, I didn't like what happened to Dean Barcomb."

She sighed. "Me either."

"I kinda suspected that too. But, I don't know, I guess I wanted to give you all a taste of your own medicine."

Audrey nodded slowly. "If you follow the blog you know we don't normally put stuff like that up." Audrey felt the need to explain herself. "It was supposed to be a fake piece but it got way out of hand."

Nick sighed. "Yeah, I guessed that. Some parts were sort of funny. But it was still a pretty crappy thing to do. I mean, what did Dean Barcomb ever do to you?"

Audrey looked down at her shoes.

"But like I said, I didn't think it all through—the anonymous texts." Nick continued, "I thought about just not showing up tonight. Or, I suppose, I could have called it off by text. But I wanted to tell you in person. It just seemed, I don't know, like the right thing to do." He shrugged. "Sounds stupid, huh?"

"No, it doesn't," Audrey said. She knew exactly how Nick felt. "So you don't really want—" she patted her hip pocket, the money practically burning a hole in her jeans.

"The two hundred? Oh no!" Nick waved his hands, chasing away the idea. "That was . . . I thought it was good payback for you saying Dean Barcomb took bribes. Like ironic or something. I never actually wanted—"

"Well, I understand," Audrey said.

"I'm really sorry I sent you those text messages," he said.

Audrey shook her head, brushing off the apology. "Let's move on," she said. "It's been a weird couple of weeks anyway. What's another crazy text or two?"

Then she had an idea and forced a casual laugh. "Oh, yeah, what'd the first one say again?" she asked. "Crazy stuff." She was almost certain Nick had nothing to do with the do-over, but she knew that *this* was her chance to find out.

"It was 'I know you wrote it. Was it fun to mess with someone's life like that? Hope so . . .'" Nick sighed. "Stupid, huh? I don't know what I was thinking."

Audrey held up her hand to stop him. "Seriously, forget it." So she still didn't know where the do-over had come from. A mystery to be solved another day, maybe. Though she seriously doubted it. There was something about a message from no number that seemed to suggest the mystery could last a lifetime.

She refocused on simpler answers. "Why are you so protective of Barcomb?" she asked. "Are you friends with Hope?"

"No, not really. She's kinda a jerk sometimes, actually. But I know what it's like to be harassed online."

Audrey blushed. "I'm sorry," she mumbled. She had written an article about internet trolls a few months ago. But Audrey hadn't realized until now that she had sort of become one herself. "It really was a stupid thing to do—the blog post. Dean Barcomb isn't a bad guy."

"No, he's not," Nick agreed.

"Yeah. You know his credentials weren't *that* fudged," Audrey continued. "Minor dates and stuff. One certificate, and he's working with the university to sort that out."

"Yeah? Where'd you hear that?" Nick asked.

"I know some people at the local paper," she said. "I think Mr. Barcomb can prove that the issues were minor, so I'm trying to convince them to do a follow-up article or something else to fix this."

"You could start a petition," he said. "At school."

"We could." She didn't know why she said it, but of course, he picked up on the slip.

"We?" He laughed. It really was a good sound.

"Yeah. If you'd be interested, I'd love your help."

Nick nodded. "Absolutely," he said. "That is, if you're not sending me to jail for blackmail or for being a super creep."

"Nah." She paused then, considered. "Are you a super creep?"

"I don't think so," he said. "At least, not before this." Now it was his turn to sigh.

"You ever wish you could go back and do it all over?"

"Yes," she said. "I do."

* * *

When she got home, there was a new text message.

This one wasn't from Nick or her friends. It was sent from a contact with no number at all.

Reply with yes if you would like to undo your do-over.

Her whole heart filled with relief. She'd never even thought, or dared, to wish for such a message. She knew exactly what her answer should be.

Yes.

«« 15

"Hello," said Audrey as brightly as she could manage.

Nick Schaeffer looked up from his book. "Oh . . ." He seemed to be struggled to process what he was seeing. He looked around the rest of the library. "Hi."

"I'm Audrey Zimmer." She held out a hand.

He shook it. "Yeah, I know. I like your articles in the school paper. I'm Nick," he said. "Nick Schaeffer."

"Nice to officially meet you," she said. "I've seen you here before, but, um, I've never taken the time to come over and say hi. I'm sorry about that."

"It's no problem. I mean, you are now." He smiled a little awkwardly, then looked around again. "Are you here with anyone?"

"No. Actually, that's what I wanted to talk with you about."

"Oh?"

"See, my friends and I run this little blog on the side—*The Espresso*."

"I've seen it," he said, eyes narrowing.

"Right. So then you know we wrote this terrible article about Dean Barcomb. And . . . well, I talked to my friends last night and finally convinced them we needed to go into Kramer's office together and admit what we did."

"Okay . . ." Nick was beyond confused. Having this conversation before any mysterious texts or burner phones or late-night apologies would do that to a person. Audrey figured this was probably a couple of days before Nick had even thought of doing something.

"We'll go into Kramer's office first thing on Monday," Audrey pressed on. "And then we're all going to be suspended."

"Wow." Nick sat up straighter, genuine concern on his face now, which really was sweet because he didn't even really know her or any of them. "That sounds rough."

"No." She shook her head, before she got completely derailed. "It's fair. We almost ruined a guy's life. But here's where we need some help. People probably won't really trust what we say about the matter after we turn ourselves in."

"Okay, sure," he said.

"And here's the thing. I've got suspicions Barcomb's credentials aren't *that* forged. Like it was just small stuff he fibbed on. I think support from the students might help his case—maybe a petition of some kind saying what a great dean he's been. Someone would need to collect all the signatures and then get it to the paper, the school board, that kind of thing."

Nick's eyes lit up. "A petition! That's a great idea."

Audrey smiled. "I thought you might be on board. And I was hoping you'd be able to carry the torch. After we come clean, we'll need someone who can . . ." Audrey thought about her next words carefully, "set things right."

"You think?" Nick still seemed a little confused, but he was coming around to the idea even if she was still a random semistranger.

"Sure," he said. "I could do that. I've always like Dean Barcomb, and getting attacked online can be pretty hard."

Audrey nodded.

"So first thing we need to do is write the petition," Nick said, opening up his laptop. "So did you . . . I mean, did you wanna get started on that now?"

"Yes," Audrey said.

ABOUT THE AUTHOR

JEFFREY PRATT studied music and English literature in college and has worked as a sports reporter, advertising copywriter, and high school English teacher. He's played guitar and piano semiprofessionally for many years. He loves the ocean, dogs, French fries, and cryptozoology. Jeff and his family split their time between Ohio and Los Angeles.